THERE IS A BRAND NEW PRESIDENT

THIS SIDE OF UTOPIA
A short story about a short revolution

Book I of The BLAK STAR Trilogy

A BRAND NEW AFRO-AMERICAN PRESIDENT...
OF AFRODESIA

THE ONLY BOOK THAT ASKS THE BIGGEST

"WHAT IF"

QUESTION OF THE 21st CENTURY!

WHAT IF AFRO-AMERICAN PEOPLE SECEDED FROM THE
UNITED STATES OF AMERICA AND ESTABLISHED THEIR
OWN SOVEREIGN NATION?

Cover Art and Illustartions by R.S. Gunn for Red Boi Design
Edited by Aiesha Turman
All rights reserved.
Copyright 2008 Shawn C Gunn
ISBN: 978-0-578-00561-4

First printing December 2008

Printed in the United States of America

For information please visit us on the World Wide Web at www.blakstartrilogy.com

FOREWORD

Meaning the word be-fore all the votes are in.

It's November 4th, 2008—Election Day. I happily stood in line for 2 hours to cast my vote. It is only 10:15 a.m. and I, like everyone else is excited to see which way it will all go tonight. I wrote these notes while standing in line at the polls and seeing all the different kinds of people this Presidential race has attracted. There is a "but" though, and it is this: as I was thinking about Barack, I was somehow reminded of Jesse Owens at the Olympic trials in Germany in 1936. Owens had taken the gold medal in the 100-meter dash the first day. The next day, Owens was to compete in the long jump. Three attempts were allowed to qualify. Owens took a practice run and was disheartened to learn that the Olympic officials overseeing the event had counted it as an attempt when they knew full well that it wasn't. He fouled out on his next try which left him with just one attempt. When the powers that be are not truly operating under the ideal of fair and equal treatment for all, it kind of makes you wonder if they should be in power. It should be noted that even though the German officials could not be called on their actions because they would simply deny they did anything wrong, it was a white man and a German (Luz Long, his biggest competition at that) who, in the true spirit of Olympic competition and wanting to compete against only the absolute best, walked over to Owens, introduced himself and suggested to Owens to simply mentally mark the spot from where he jumped to ensure he would not foul out on the last attempt. Long understood that you can not consider yourself the best until you have beaten the best fair and square. And for all you fans of Babe Ruth, his legacy as one of baseball's greatest will always be suspect knowing that a guy like Josh Gibson in the Negro Leagues even existed. Josh played in the same era, but never had his chance to duel against Ruth because he was excluded from the Major Leagues based solely on the color of his skin, but that's another debate for another day. Owens won the long jump gold medal and Long congratulated him.

Afro-people say this and that about the Rev. Dr. Martin Luther King Jr. and The Honorable Minister Malcolm X and many others from the civil rights movement giving their lives so that Afro-people might have the right to vote among other civil rights. Yet, if they were alive and here today I believe they would even say that their struggle was for us to achieve ALL our Human rights and fair and equal treatment. The process of this election has shown me we are moving forward but in baby steps. The correlation between Jesse Owens and Barack relates to an ideology that Afro-people have become accustom to, and that is Afro-people have to work twice as hard to get half as much. Nothing against white people, but definitely something against white privilege and white supremacy. Some may call this cynical, I call it a reality check. If Barack wins tonight and is voted into Office as the first Afro-American President ever, I will not jump for joy or go crazy in the streets, but I will have a huge grin from ear to ear for a few moments. After that I know the real work will begin for him and his battle will be ALL uphill. How much unnecessary B.S., antagonistic behavior, and back-biting tricks meant to slow the momentum of positive change is this man going to have to navigate his way through or endure if he is elected?

Everyone is entitled to their own opinions, that is one of the principals this country was supposedly founded on. However, facts belong to everyone and no one is entitled to his or her version of them. If you analyze the players in this Presidential game, you have an Ivy League educated, articulate, charismatic, well-credentialed man of color. He is pitted against a doddering, old white man with one foot in the grave and a white woman who has been declared by most (including a large constituent of White women) as being as dumb as a box of rocks. Fact: As of a month ago this race shouldn't have even been considered close.

The playing field for Afro-people in relation to the powers that be is not level yet. Win or Lose, there is a glimmer of hope that my Children or Grandchildren will experience it - Completely.

THIS SIDE OF UTOPIA

A short story about a short revolution

Book I of The BLAK STAR Trilogy

Satire \sa-,tir\ n: biting wit, irony or sarcasm used to expose vice or folly.

It's Nation Time.

And this time, "The Revolution Will Be Televised". We have no other choice since most people are inside watching t.v. more than they are outside communing with nature or interacting with each other.

Check your local listings for time, date, and network.
Written by: S.C. Gunn
Started at 9 a.m. Tuesday June 19, 2007
Completed at 2 p.m. Tuesday November 04, 2008

Today marks the dawn of a new day for so-called "Black people" here in America. The birth of a golden age. A step out of the darkness into the light. We have now embarked upon a journey to the promised land of mental, spiritual, and emotional liberation and the freedom to truly control one's own destiny, not to mention financial bliss. The ways and means of all this joy comes from a power resource that we, for the time being, seem to have in great abundance and if things remain as they are, even for some time to come, appears to be inexhaustible. The resource is something that we were sitting on all along and that others have seen fit to profit from in the past while we stood by and let them. The resource is us. This short manifesto is a "Modest Proposal" of sorts to diagram the methods and practices we the new Afro Nation plan to employ to maintain a happy and healthy relationship primarily amongst ourselves, but also with other nations around the world.

The melanin we possess, along with what we will call here, the Nine-ether trait has been at the center of great debate lately because it has been discovered that there is a special intrinsic value hidden within these bio-chemical miracles, especially if extracted from around the scalp area near the frontal lobe. This has become a high commodity.

Every type of Afro person from someone as high-yellow as former Miss America Vanessa Williams or actor Terence Howard to a person as blue-black as Flava Flav or the late Great Miles Davis and every shade in between has become a potential source of energy replacing crude oil from the Middle East as the main type of world energy. The other big hoo-rah is that so-called "Black" people have just gained their independence from white people in the United States and created their own sovereign nation with a long awaited and very belated reparations re-payment for the atrocities of the Middle Passage Slave Trade here in the Americas. Afro-people were given thirteen states along the Western Coast, everything from Seattle, Washington down to El Segundo. We are so elated to now have our own starter-kit, D.I.Y. Country. The name of the new land is AFRODISIA.

The one fear our new Afrodisian intellectual elite are concerned about now is that we will piss everything away and go from having everything to nothing in the snap of a finger. They want to know do we have enough skilled laborers to support the new nation as a whole. Are the amount of professionals proportional to the number of citizens that need their expertise? The sick will need doctors, roads will need to be built, hospitals and other buildings erected. Agricultural advances will need to be made, as well as ecologically sound waste management and conservation. Their concern that we could become an instant third world nation due to our lack of scientific knowledge, not to mention the political process on the Federal, State, or Local government level is not unfounded. Masters in all disciplines are needed, but especially Engineers (Civil and Mechanical), Scientists, Accountants, Mathematicians, and Statisticians and we are in great need of teachers of mathematics and the sciences. They are in very very high demand in this new world and will be paid accordingly.

Our melanin has always been a mystery to most along with the Nine-ether in one's body that causes hair follicles to curl into the shape of the number nine. Which must mean we are divine people since nine is the most complete and divine number. Yet, for the last century or so and maybe even longer, so-called "Black" people have been trying to come up with ways to straighten our hair. Our popular entertainers dating back to Nat King Cole and Duke Ellington somehow "Processed" their naturally curly hair to be slicked back and contrary to what anyone says, any cosmetic changes done to one's person is most often for the sole purpose of attracting the opposite sex—why people spend time trying to deny this I will never understand. The more pertinent question is how did torturing one's own head become a mean to and end in being considered sexy? Our Afro women even had gone so far as to perfect a new process of sewing other people's hair (possibly dead people) onto their own heads. To please who and to look like what?

The new energy resource we've discovered is extracted from several key points on the body, but mostly from the front of the scalp, it has been noted that Afro men now make better subjects than Afro women. This is due to the fact of most Afro women's hair and scalp is often times scorched and clogged with all kinds of chemicals and goop that suffocates the pores on her head, therefore making her head barren of any of the nutrients and natural juices needed to create this new energy source. Some "Black" women say their hair is that way because they don't have time to take care of their Crowning Glory properly, so they go for the quick fix due to the facts, "mama gotta get on her grind 'cause baby need a new pair of shoes and papa done flew da' coup." Even though they drop a lot of money on these concoctions, for the most part they still look like shit most of the time and Afro men in the old American world just didn't have the balls to say it to the women's faces. Not that it would matter very much if they did. I'm not a hair expert by any stretch of the imagination, but wouldn't common sense and logic tell a woman that if we are all living, breathing, organisms and need oxygen like everything else, why would you take something dead or an inanimate synthetic and sew it into something that's alive for long stretches of time? That's like putting something dead on top of something alive and expecting positive results. As if the thing underneath, your hair!, will still be healthy. Picture very experienced, nimble fingers helping weave long, artificial dead strands of hair around living, breathing, healthy strands of hair and choking off air, maybe a bit over-exaggerated, but you understand. Looks good when it's in, but it's when they have to take it out, unbraid and pull apart the fake from the real, you see the way the natural hair looks violated, tangled and twisted with caked-up hair oil and sometimes glue in pockets. I saw a heavy-set "Black" woman come out of a beauty salon the other day and some Brother yelled to her, "Hey baby-girl, yo' hair sho' look nice." She grinned from ear to ear. The only question I had was, "You paid somebody to do that?" It looked like an over-turned cuckoos nest… Whatever works for you? But I might have thought, if she got out of the chair, looked in the mirror and saw her head like that, the hairdresser might have suffered severe consequences and repercussions, instead she was seemingly satisfied. Her head was a spectacle of many, many, tiny, black and copper colored braids pulled back into a pony-tail. It kind of looked like a psychedelic, Davie Crocket Raccoon hat. For most Afro-American women, weaving extra hair into their own was no longer a style in old America. It was a life style. The one exception to the rule would be an actress or a model either preparing for a role or getting ready to display a character in a photo shoot. It wasn't like wearing a hair clip, a ribbon, a bow, a flower or even a fancy hat. You can take those off at the end of the day. We here in the new world identify the problem as the act of self mutilation, thinking the natural hair on your head is perpetually and inherently ugly which couldn't be further from the truth. The good-hair, bad-hair thing was drilled into their sub-conscious so hard and deep by not only radio, music videos, and television advertising, but was usually started by mama, aunt-tee-tee, older sister and shamefully—especially the so-called "Black" man. So much so that it prompted the woman to set aside money and schedule out large blocks of time to, not enhance the hair that was there, but try to pretty it up to look like what was considered the norm—with bone straight or flowing locks being the norm. Humph...? One of the funniest sights you'd ever see was an Afro Lady the first night after she's had an appointment with the hairdresser and she has some special occasion or function to go to the next day. She'll sleep with her hair covered by a doo-rag and her head propped up with one hand all night, so as not to spoil the new doo by resting her head on a pillow. How much her wrist hurt the next morning was completely dependent upon how big her head was. Or even funnier were the ghetto girls who play their heads like bongo drums because they don't want to loosen their weave job with their fingernails, so when their scalp itched they'd pat their heads really hard. If the itch became really bothersome, some chicks looked as if they were going to knock their own brains out. I'd been told to vacate the premises on more than one occasion because when they started doing this, I would go into my Ricky Riccardo routine and start singing BAABAA-LOOOOO! Afro-American, Afro-African, and Dominican hairdressers along with Korean cosmetic store owners in old America raked in millions of dollars yearly from our Afro women who bought hair in a bag (or something that looked like hair) and charged them upwards of $80 for it then at least $100 more to a hairdresser to install it. We here in the new nation know all of this was a result of the idea that there was shame in wearing their own natural hair because white people in the old world had brainwashed us all into thinking the more European we looked the better we were as people. I suppose the phrase that fits here is "Might makes Right" and it's not surprising to us that a lot of the world holds European countries and their cultures in high regard when Africa is just as fascinating, if not more-so. People plan vacations to visit and explore various European historical monuments and sites. It's also not surprising that European nations hold most of the world's war weapons. Translation, our culture is the biggest and the baddest because we kick some major ass around here and if you want to be like us, first you have to look like us. Well, getting our dark skin to look white, that might pose a problem. Reminder: call Michael Jackson this afternoon and see how he's recovering from that last operation. Sad as the situation was, when it came to profits, I don't even think the Afro-American hair-care companies made out as good as white owned companies. Furthermore, with just a little investigative research you'd discover that some of the companies you thought were Afro-American owned, really had an all white corporate board of directors with so-called "Black" folk just minding the store as a front. It just goes to prove you can sell people almost anything even the idea that they are ugly or a part of them is ugly and that you have a $180 remedy that will beautify them when in actuality they were beautiful all along.

We, the proud Afro men of the new Nation, ask that you all please accept our humble apology for any old backwards ideas and actions our fellow Brothers of the old American mind-state took part in. To our women and children, we are truly sorry. The founders of the new Nation seek to rectify the wrongs by discipline, mobilization, and education of the masses. And oh, how we love our fine, proud, Afro Queens and Princesses in the new Nation with their healthy, greased scalps and natural braids or perfectly coiffed afros, worn like a glorious crown.

Note to self: Call stock broker after this and cop some more shares of Afro-Sheen.

In our new world the first order of business is to execute all Niggers, Nigger sympathizers and those who display Nigger-ish behavior. We'll bring them to the town squares in every village and town and let 'em have it right in front of everybody as an example of what we are not going for here in the new world. Now let's clarify what is meant by the word Nigger for the record. I will paraphrase William Faulkner, to put it into context. The term Nigger I use does not refer just to what we know as so-called "Black" people. To be quite honest, I see so-called "white" people acting like Niggers all the time, only the American community at large does not define it as such. Here's a good example: a rag-tag bunch of low-lives and unsavory characters board a boat in England (rumor has it that they were kicked out, but I have no way of confirming this since I wasn't there) floated over here to what we now call the Americas, dug what they saw then off'ed almost all of the Native people on this land then threw a flag down and called the land their own. They liberated the land so-to-speak from the savages. It only makes me wonder who the savages really were? That type of thing happens in the ghetto all the time—somebody beats you up, takes your shit (or liberates it) and dares you to ask for it back. Now if that ain't a Nigger, I don't know what is.

This new Nation must have a gross national product to open up trade relations with other nations. Seeing how Afro people are good at entertainment—Sports, Music, Acting, etc.—I guess that would fall under the category of a service trade. But we will need some form of a raw material, a product that will help our new nation's economy thrive. Our new scientific discovery is the Holy Grail for our fiscal success as a young country. This magical, chemical compound found within the Nine-ether and melanin in Afro people's skin and bones is being dissected and cataloged in labs across the country as we speak. Afro-people have a genetic trait that houses this sort of "soul power" energy which is not easily detected, even with the use of the world's most powerful microscopes, but it is identifiable when the subject is exposed to the sun. The exposure initiates a chain reaction that activates and unlocks stored energy encased within our genetic code. A hundred subjects may yield ten gallons of the new liquefied "black gold". One gallon of this new source of energy could power an entire town for a month. This has become a source of energy more valuable than crude oil. Yet, it looks like oil, smells like oil, but it's not oil. The one caveat is the extraction process is so intense that it causes donor to expire within hours, it's like Kemo-therapy cranked up to turbo boost. Workers at the extraction factory affectionately refer to the combine as "The Juicer". Death Row inmates from the old world and some of our own serious offenders from our new society are our main donor resource. Of course we look forward to the day when we'll have no crime or criminals in our midst, but for right now we have enough persons of ill repute to keep the entire God fearing, law abiding portion of our population living like movie stars, driving big cars, drinking Crystál and eating caviar for at least 3 or 4 generations. The days of birthing a nation full of a big bunch of doe-does is long past and by the time my great-great-grand kids are running things, the smarty-pants we are creating will think of some other ways for our still new Nation to turn a profit.

The process for producing this new energy source was discovered a long time before the new Afro Nation gained it's independence from white America by white scientists doing experiments on "Black" subjects in a few American Federal and State prisons. Just like the notes the American scientists made a deal for during the end of World War II with the Japanese doctors who had conducted sick, inhumane experiments on their own people and prisoners of war, Afro doctors and scientists had to beg for the notes on the experiments white doctors and scientists had conducted because for years they denied that the experiments even existed and kept their findings a well hidden secret.

One of the white scientists, who at one time was the head coordinator of the tests, had been demoted from his position as the leader of the project because some of his ideas started to clash with the financial backers and his fellow scientists on the project. He eventually got angry and disenchanted with the overall direction of the project and removed himself from any further experiments, eventually dropping out of the research program all together or maybe he was asked to leave? Whichever was the case, after his departure from the program, he was followed by the CIA off and on and he knew it. Yet, that didn't stop him from contacting the new Nation's scientists to inform them of the valuable notes he possessed and that he could give them other crucial information for a set price. The original price he asked for was $80 million. The new Nation's scientists had to go to their government officials and certain powerful big business bankers who had political interests in the matter to explain how and why this information was crucial to have and that the knowledge of how to tap this hidden energy source could help give their economy a much needed boost. There were months of haggling back and forth, but alas the Afro scientists received the money from their government. Once the exchange of money for information was made, the white scientist decided to move his family to the new Afro Nation for a while, mainly for safety reasons. He wasn't quite sure if the American government was still monitoring his movements at this point, but he had a strong suspicion even if they weren't they would start again now.

His wife never knew about the experiments until he (the white scientist) had to explain how he came into so much money all at once and why they needed to move their family. Shortly after the sale of the information, the white scientist took a job at a university in the new Nation as a professor of Forensic science. It was an added plus that the new Nation offered his family a lower cost of living with very little change to their standard of living.

He and his family set up shop in their new palatial home and fell into a daily routine. He had few new friends, so he would usually just come straight home from work every day. Fridays, he would stay a few extra hours to go over student papers and other work. One Friday night, well after 11 p.m., his wife starts to worry and just as she reaches to pick up the phone to call the police—it rings. It's her husband. He sounds fine and he says he's ok. She repeatedly asks him when he will be home? There is a long silence. He says, "I love you. I always will. Tell the children their dad loves them with all his heart." He rushes to tell her where more money is stashed and that she should not try to move. "You and the kids are fine. Just promise me you will stay there." She wants to know what is going on? "Where are you?", her high-pitched voice begs into the receiver. She now realizes she's on the phone alone. He's gone. He must be at a pay phone, there is street noise in the background. All she hears now are car and bus engines as they rumble and hum back and forth. Horns honk. Sirens whine. She never sees her husband again.

The scientists of the new Nation take the information and pour over it day in and day out for months. The project for a long time is top secret. But soon the results of the work start to leak throughout the small, but ever-growing new Nation's scientific community. At the same time, the new Afro government was trying to figure out a way to de-program the so-called "Black" people from the old ways they used to think when Afro-people were a part of America. They asked themselves how do we rid ourselves of the old thought processes that caused our people to not care about their own communities or the individual men and women of prime age, elderly, and children within them and even worse to become so dependent on white ingenuity, organization, and technological advancements rendering the entire race a majority of consumers instead of producers? There was an overall unhealthy relationship between Afro people and white people in old America, a co-dependency with Afro people getting the worse end of the deal because even though they collectively were brilliant, they always seem to seek approval from white people. The so-called "Black" people of old America didn't even have a National bank to call their own. Those among them who were smart and professionally skilled (if they wanted any kind of financial security for themselves and their immediate families) had no other choice but to have all their efforts co-opted by white people and used to further the advancement of the white community, leaving the Afro community in a sort of suspended animation or more succinctly, a state of arrested development. To put it more plainly, instead of the crabs figuring out how to create prosperity within the barrel they always felt the need to climb out and once successfully out the other crabs would run a guilt trip on them if they didn't reach back to help a few more climb out, and shamefully, a lot actually wanted you back in the barrel if they couldn't figure a way out for themselves. The old American so-called "Black" folk always seemed to be playing to the lowest common denominator.

We needed to clear out the abundance of prisons and prisoners we had so we could turn some of those facilities into places of higher learning instead of so-called rehabilitation. We as a new nation took it upon ourselves to get in front of the crime problem and eliminate the causes of criminal activity in our own community, not just sit on our hands and make adjustments to the effects after-the-fact. A lot of times in the old world, so-called "Black" folks would turn to others outside their community for help with things like "Black" on "Black" crime. Our men here in the new world see that action as very effeminate. There's nothing more pathetic, figuratively speaking, than a man taking his balls off and handing them to another man. It's as if to say, "I can't handle problems in my own house, woe is me, please help me". So, that is why criminals have become our primary source of test material. You kill (no pun intended) two birds with one stone, you get rid of the State's criminal element and at the same time you create revenue for the young country's economy.

In our new nation, most drugs are legal. Money that was previously earmarked for that fake-ass war on drugs bullshit that the white American government was running is now used on Rehab centers, abuse prevention programs and youth job skill training.

Prostitution is legal also and governed by our CDC and MDA (Council for Disease Control and Medical Doctors Association). All the women and what few man-whores there are must pass a monthly physical. The government does not regulate prices for pleasure services, but workers will be required to keep strict records of every transaction and pay taxes to the state, federal, and city municipalities for the privilege to do what they do.

If a person is found to be infected with as little as the common cold they will not be allowed to work until ok'd by a board certified Medical Doctor. If this rule is violated, swift and immediate criminal prosecution will be administered. The severity of the punishment will be strictly based on the severity of the sickness they have passed on. Of course if you have knowingly or unknowingly infected someone with a fatal disease like HIV, there will be no questions asked. If it's traced back to you—Death Penalty.

While we're on the subject of capital punishment, I think I speak for everyone here in the new Nation when I say we do not derive any joy from the murder of any of our Brothers and Sisters. Yet, those of us who remember the ways of so-called "Black" folk in the old America remember the pain and suffering we could bring to each other. The intellectuals here in our new nation observed and identified those actions long ago as what is referred to in clinical psychology as Transference. Eldridge Cleaver once wrote that oppressed people rarely attack their oppressors, instead they attack each other. For example, if I have an Afro brother who's my friend, who looks like me and has the same background as me, and we both have to answer to the white man's legislation and laws and abide by whatever it is that he lays down even if it doesn't benefit us, we become angry at the white man, but we have short patience and tolerance with each other and take out our aggression and hate that should be more aptly directed at someone who is trying to stunt our progress (and/or relegate us to a sub-standard of living), on one another. We hold each other in such low disregard because deep down we are both a couple of pussies who ultimately won't stand together to stand up for what's fair and right and ride or die to defend it. And to every so-called "Black" man reading this now—YOU TOO!

Listen closely to some of the lyrics of those "gangsta rappers". You very rarely heard them reserve violence for anyone but another Afro person whether they be man or woman. Those youth that enjoyed hearing all that rah-rah needed to check a few dudes, but they were too weak-minded and equated criminal behavior with bravery. That was the most dangerous thing we discovered about the mind-set of the old world Afro youth. Some of those recording geniuses, the hardrocks, were typical street cats, but contrary to popular belief there were a lot from two parent suburban homes who had the propensity to be studio gangsters. You'd see the pink panties underneath all their skirts if you ever spoke to them about real gang-bangin' of a revolutionary kind on a geo-political level. This is not to say we don't understand from where the complacency derives. The way the white man's political system governed old America, it caused an imbalance of power to the detriment of Afro-people which often times created a situation in where any poor person who sought to change a law that was unfair to them may be accused of breaking said law, but a politician or corporate executive who broke the law might be looked upon as a maverick who seeks to change the law. Term limits for mayor of New York City were set at two terms equaling eight years, but one mayor decided to buck the entire Democratic process and re-elected himself to be put on the ballot for a third term in office. He bulldozed the issue right past a vote by the people of the city to a referendum vote by a committee he knew would see things in his favor. Absolute power corrupts absolutely. One American president even gave American taxpayer's money to bail out a bunch of rich guys who fucked-over a lot of Americans money in the housing market instead of giving it to the people who were losing their homes because of outright greed and negligence on the part of big business. Insult to injury and more injury. Still, we found it funny how even the most hardened thugs cut a conversation short about political things going on right in their own neighborhood. Some didn't know the names of their Alder-persons or city council representatives nor even bothered to find out, let alone show up for a city council meeting about things being decided on their own block. The typical response was, "Aww, man I don't know." They didn't know and didn't want to know because knowing would mean they might have to act and according to the streets and the music that reflects what goes on in the streets all "Black" thugs want to do is go for the easy out which is not to pick on Goliath, but try to punk other Davids' like himself, someone on their same level. Even Stevie Wonder could see an Afro man who murdered another Afro man got a lot less time than if he attacked someone white. In cases of "Black on "Black" crime, liberal defense council for some of these thugs would have the audacity to use the product-of-their-environment card as an excuse for murder. Here in the new Nation we ain't going for it, every life has potential in our eyes and is precious up to a point and that point is when you murder your brother or sister.

Last century's Million Man March was the only thing that even came close to Afro men acting like MEN, but not much changed from then til now. It is an admonition here in the new Nation that Afro men of old America as a collective were so dumb that they didn't see all the injustices against them and as a group, they just chose to turn a blind eye to it. Yet, if something really horrific happened there would be marches in the streets and movements and rallies set up to include other races of people, but there never seemed to be that one issue where Black men just stood up and put their foot down and said "No more" or "You will not do this here." In the ghetto you have "Black" gangs and rap crews that stand in allegiance over bullshit—diamond studded chains with record label names or gang name tattoos. Yet, if you were to ask those same dudes, "hey let's go march down to City Hall and demand job training and jobs for young dudes in the hood" or challenge the pack-of-lies, white-washed history books that were still being used in public schools to teach our children, all of a sudden the Nigga's heart starts pumping Kool-aid. The army, the navy, the marines, the CIA, the FBI, the NSA, the court system, the police, the board of education—all that power governed by white people and for all the fire-breathing and wolf-ticket-selling brothers sometimes do, we all know who runs the show, or as we see it, who used to run the show. The so-called "Black" man in old America knew what time it was. So-called "Black" folk back then may have acted buck-ass crazy with each other, but they weren't stupid or at least not when it came to confronting white folks. If you looked at the police blotter in any local "Black" community across America on any given weekend, Friday thru Sunday, especially in summer, you'd sometimes see a staggering amount of murders related to narcotics sales which proves that the Afro men of the old world weren't afraid to kill or at least not the people in their own communities. Some of us in the new Nation old enough to remember, experienced the severe the lack of respect so-called "Black" people had for one another first-hand in the old world and we want no part of it here. We take the safety and well-being of the citizens in our community very seriously. Another thing we found troubling was Afro-people in old America used to get so uptight when a white cop killed an Afro man. But when it was an Afro person killing an Afro officer of the law or even another Afro citizen, there were no marches, no protest, and no outrage. We here in the new world were saddened by that. It's as if you had an entire people who had no regard for authority or the life or their brothers and sisters. That is something we absolutely WILL NOT, under any circumstances, tolerate. Our police here are Afro-people like you and are here to protect Afro-people. You harm or kill them—we kill you. And if you have family members that survive you, they will have a price to pay for your actions as well. First off, they will be charged for the executioner's day of pay and the cost of the bullet used to dispatch you.

The content aired on a channel like BET has become obsolete here because people are doing their best to change the social cues and conditions that trigger Nigger behavior which is a prominent staple of this television network; a network, by-the-way, that was eventually completely owned by a white conglomerate company. Picture that, a white company in control of the transmission worldwide of images of Afro people? And Afro people in the old world stood around and allowed it. Powerless to stop it. And not only that, they had the audacity, the temerity, the unmitigated gall to hold conferences and symposiums(usually in rented auditoriums and lecture halls owned by white people) on how to project a more positive image of Afro-people - IN THE BROADCAST MEDIA! With Afro-people owning less than 1% of broadcast and internet media companies? And what we discovered is even if Afro people had graduated to owning their own film companies and television networks they would still be at the mercy of the white man because in old America, he still owned the transmission systems and satellites that tracked across the sky and beamed radio frequencies all over the globe to all types of devices cell phones, laptops, audio/video receivers. We here in the new Nation own two satellites. We believe in total and absolute self sufficiency for our people and total self determination which means freedom to project one's true self without some other culture filtering out whatever they deem objectionable or filtering in what we deem objectionable. Funny how Malcolm X in one of his last speeches given long ago spoke of the media as tool for the governmental establishment and how those who run it can shape a story and the people within the story any way they see fit. If an entire community is reported as being bad, then the people within it, even if they are good, can be easily framed as bad. For example, a victim of police brutality can be made to look like a victimizer, the sentiment being, "He or she must have done something wrong, resisted arrest, something? An officer of the law wouldn't just shoot an innocent person." They would if they are not from that community, don't know the people, don't look like the people, don't care about the people, have been conditioned to be afraid of the people, and most importantly don't understand the people and lastly don't live in, around, or near that community and don't have to see or deal with the residual effects of their brutality on the person and their family. There were some commercial t.v. networks in old America that did make an honest effort to bring positive Afro-people content to the masses, but a lot of times all the effort was good for was creating corporate sponsored lust for products that most Afro-people couldn't afford anyway and when they weren't doing that they were just creating lust (.)

I digress. I've gotten off on a tangent, back to the subject at hand. The worth of the melanin compound has become very valuable. In fact, over the next few years it will become the MOST valuable worldwide commodity.

Former Afro-Americans, the descendants of slaves, are considered the new Arabs of the West now that the melanin compound has replaced oil as the world's energy source. There is only one catch: in order to extract this biological compound from the blood cells and bone marrow of the subjects the process has to be ignited by nuclear fission. Which gives the new republic an excuse to construct its own reactor—for energy purposes of course. ;-)

The citizens of this new Nation have their education from Pre-School to Grad School paid in full by the government. The government also foots the bill for all its citizens health care and to answer your first question, "No. The services are not shabby or cut-rate." The educators are top notch and the doctors are all well educated, the best in their respective areas of medical practice.

The first important campaign the government sponsors is a nation wide literacy campaign. There is a mandate by the government and the country's educators to wipe out illiteracy.

In accordance with all this cultural upheaval, the constructors of the new Nation took into account that Hip-Hop music played a major role in so-called "Black culture" at the end of the 20th century leading into the new 21st century, or new millennium. Afrodesian intellects were all up-in-arms over what to do about the use of degrading, foul language most often times referring not to whites, but right back at Afro-people themselves. There was even an uproar that focused on "Black" Rappers and their language, but get this, it started out with the firing of a white man from a radio station who was pretending to play a hip, jive, "Black" hip-hop character, only this white man let his big, alligator mouth get his humming bird ass in a lot of hot water with other powerful white people. Still haven't figured that one out yet? Just like back in the late 1980's when a television network fired sports commentator Jimmy-The-Greek for a comment he made about

"Black" athletes, mostly white people got uptight. I didn't see many Afro-people reacting to what he said. When he was caught on camera mentioning the unmentionable, poor Jimmy seemed to be more than a little toasted at the time and may have exposed some things he heard discussed in sports network backrooms at board meetings—opinions corporate whites wanted to keep covered, as if we couldn't see them anyway. Maybe they feared if their true thoughts and feeling were exposed there would be a mass boycott by all Afro athletes causing an economic fall-out in the sports industry. Hey, economic boycott. That ain't a half bad idea… But, peep how the white media conglomerates with the help of so-called "Black" political leaders and television personalities shifted the focus of the controversy. The white radio host poked fun at a mostly Afro woman's volleyball team and referred to them as, "A scary lookin' bunch a bitches with arm pits and legs so hairy they all looked like cousins of King Kong", "One of 'em had so much armpit hair, it looked like she had Buckwheat in a headlock", and " Them Stank Ho's couldn't pull a chain saw through their nappy heads." He and his side-kick laughed, guffaw-guffaw, and continued. But this next joke indicated to me that "Black" people weren't the only ones up watching those stupid late night comedy shows on "Black" Entertainment Television, I don't think a conservative stick-up-his-ass white man could think of a joke like this. He said, one the players Lesley Swopes "had hair so nappy, her ears bought a gun." And went on, "Yeah, and when I say stank, I mean stank! The stench from that B.O. in their locker room could probably be bottled and used as a new form of smelling salts, whew-weee!" then his side-kick chimes in, "And a couple of 'em look like they could use a shave." They both were really laughin'-it-up. I thought to myself, "Sheeeshh! Where's the love, daddy!?" Anyway, the day ended and no one thought anymore of it until the next day when the stuff-hit-the-fan; it was all over the newspaper headlines and on the 24 hr. news channels. "Stank Ho's"? "Nappy headed"? A white man said this? All kind of "Black" political leaders weighed in on the subject and it only took about a week, but before long the angle of view shifted right back to our own beloved, dear "Black" rappers, especially the gangster rappers. You know, the ones with the defiant songs and the videos with the light skinned, long haired (some of it's fake they tell me) Afro girls with nice, big, pillowy, rippley, booties in thongs or Daisey-Duke shorts. Although, now I see a few smart-asses placing white women in those videos skanking around and shaking that ass and they actually have one! Not like the old days where they were mostly all flat. They still have a problem with the rhythm and dancing thing though. Afro women beware!: you all should know that an Afro man's lust for a light skinned Afro woman is just a veiled attempt to covet the white man's blonde haired, blue eyed prize, kind of like having a woman with soul in a white wrapper or as close to white as he can get. No disrespect to our light skinned sisters. Yet, if this thing with white girls starting to grow asses like Afro women continues, well, let's just say things might get a bit more interesting in race relations. And Lord only knows what might happen if they learn to dance? For now though, Beyonce can rest easy with the fact that neither Jessica Simpson nor Britney Spears' stage show will never even come close to hers. But, what I'm layin'-in-the-cut waiting to see is how long the white man puts up with dogg-black, gutter, Negroes debasing their precious run away brides in such a pubic{sic} (I'm sorry) I mean public way or maybe I'm just way too old fashioned and a new day has dawned without me knowing—but I don't think so. The songs they rapped about spoke of marijuana use, purple haze, liquor and a number of other formerly illegal substances they used to escape the reality that before the raper {sic}, Damnit, I mean rapper started rapping, he or she was poor and life was just plain fucked up. Now there is plenty of money and he or she gets high not to escape, but just because they're a creature of habit and it feels good, sort of like masturbation, it feels good too, but produces nothing useable—only a momentary sensation. Then there's the big ballers talking about their million dollar estates in the Hamptons. And boy, how I wish I had a red-boned, light skinned gal with long hair, cute face, big butt, and a million dollar shack in the Hamptons with a Rolls Royce, Phantom and a white Chauffeur named Bently. All right, knock it off, stop screwin' around and snap out of it.

So-called "Black" people and white people alike validate "Black" rappers acting like Niggers. We buy the product. We're addicted to it, we breath it, we eat it, we drink it, we ring tone it, we like it, we love it, we smoke, snort, sniff it. We gotta have it. We help them get Nigger-Rich and build Nigger-Rich empires of shoe, clothing and soft-drink product endorsement deals based on the projection of an idiotic life style that promotes the glorification of animalistic behavioral cues borne out of circumstance of abject poverty and old world Afro men rolled all this stupid shit up into one idea called "Keepin' it Real" . The rich, so-called "entertainment entrepreneurs" might look at the attitude we have towards their behavior here in the new Nation and call us a bunch of "Haters" and our reply, "Takes one to know one." To have your creative muse spew out the amount of vile violence projected right back at anyone who looks just like you takes an immense amount of self hate and if you read the thing a few pages back about Transference you know you're a coward too. The State takes serious notice of these entertainers because they are icons that people look up to and they set an example for the rest of us. We believe strongly that the cult of personality is a very strong influence. Think of the most popular rappers we have had. Without naming names, all have children. A couple of them have love children with women they keep quiet with child support and most likely other money, but none are married and as much they don't like it, I will expose it—no matter what you read or are told all the top money earners in rap are about 40. But now 30's the new 15 or whatever it is they say. The thing that stops most hetero-sexual Afro men from marriage is the fear and frustration that they will not be able to financially support a family and most cannot, or at least not by a standard that we have come to understand as comfortable. And seeing how the entire society of the old world is driven by the need to get their hands on disposable income to buy a bunch of stuff to keep up with the Jones's. If you don't have enough bread, even if your Afro woman accepts you, she may look down on you for one reason or another which may cause your relationship strife, but the real reason will be you just don't have enough money. One major reason is that statistics showed in the old world Afro women graduated from college at a rate of about 5 to 1 in comparison to their Afro male counter-parts. And not many women want to marry a man who is a dummy, unless he's a rich dummy. I must point out that this is not all women, but too many. The Afro woman in the old world was placed in a precarious position if she had true love for brothers. Her choices were limited to Afro-men who were broke and still looked to act like the man in charge and control her life which actually could hold her back, but even worse this kind of relationship resembles more of a Mother/Child relationship where

She is the bread-winner and gives Him money and a lot of Afro women were very understanding when it came to this, but in a way it is kind of pathetic to see a woman coddling a grown man and it's no wonder why a lot of these relationships never lasted. Unfortunately, a lot lasted long enough to produce a child or children and ill advice on relationships is passed down and ill behaviors toward the opposite are adopted. Usually at some point after the honeymoon period of the relationship has worn off, the woman grows tied of (for lack of a better term) "wearing the balls" in the relationship. It's fun in the beginning, but any real feminine woman wants the man to be a man and take care of things. If she has to give him money under the table or on the low to go take care of things, that will play out eventually. The other scenario is she meets an Afro man with education and/or money who has options and by options, I mean if he's got money, even if you are Fine Fine and blow his mind, if you are constantly rocking the boat with insecurity issues (most commonly by talking too much and arguing) he may have other women to go to. He could Love you til the ends of the earth, but just not be able to handle the negative energy you're putting out and that cuts both ways because there are some brothers that bring bad energy to the table as well. "Daddy issues" and with careful study and analysis of our Afro brothers and sisters in the old world we found both the Afro-man and Afro-woman were equally effected by this in different ways which created a ticking time bomb when most got together as Man and Woman couples. American custom dictated that most Afro women in a serious relationship with a man looked to have that relationship exclusive to only them. Yet, the more money he has, the more options that are open to him and if he's charismatic, cultured, and good-looking (and sometimes money does wonders for one's looks) it may be a wrap on the "The boy is mine" notion. That doesn't mean he acts upon those options and any woman reading this DO NOT go off on a tangent and think there are no monogamous, good, family-minded Afro men out here, be they poor or rich. Yet, it must be said some of us Afro men also lack the mental and emotional capabilities to support a family, but then again, so do some of our women. A healthy mind state, capable of giving love and support to children and establishing goals and expectations is a process that has to be instilled in youth from their parents at a young age. If the madness of irresponsibility and un-accountability trickles down from the Elders of a Nation, your people are on a collision course with disaster. It all starts with the man-woman relationship. Yes, a man looks for a woman to possess physical beautiful and Yes, a woman looks for a man to have financial security, but somehow these natural inclinations got distorted to a superficial extreme in old America. And here is where the danger lies, each man and woman have their own definition of what those things mean to them and those ideas should be discussed and cultivated by people in your own community that share your same core values and interests. When you have outside forces of other cultures influencing you, un-realistic ideas of beauty like say, Afro women chemically wrestling their naturally curly Afro hair into submission to look Spanish, Italian or Indian or a Afro boy thinking if he doesn't become some type of major star with money he is not a success or he is less than, both the idea of beauty and financial security become polluted.

Of course every man fears being tied down to one woman when there are so many available fine, Afro women, but that is not as big an issue as one might think. Money is the main thing. And these star rappers (at least according to what they say in their music) have money out the ass. They have beautiful women whom have had children for them. Are these women not worthy of marriage? Maybe the women they've had kids with are all bat-shit crazy? Or maybe.... Naaahhh... with all that big talk of beatin' Niggas up, jail time, rock slangin', bustin' guns, weed smoke and liquor. They all gotta be He-Men. I'd bet the farm on it.

Yet, sports stars are the worst when it comes to this. Almost every week there is a paternity suit filed against this Afro athlete or that one. It's also strange (again not naming names) that when you see interview footage of an Afro athletes after winning an important game or a championship you'd see their mothers overjoyed, jumping around in the picture like a bunch of banshees! And very rarely, if ever, do you see an Afro athlete's father. Hmmm? Not that the mothers shouldn't be proud of their son's accomplishments, but not only where is the man's father, but where is the wife? Even worse is sometimes these mothers would overstep their boundaries and open their big mouths to the media when the guy (if he's a big enough star) has a publicist to help him navigate his way through negotiations with management or problems with the team. An utterly ridiculous sight to see is when an athlete's mom has the gumption to run out onto a court or field full of grown men gladiators if she feels someone has hurt her two-hundred-and-some-odd-pounds-six foot-something, baby (or her golden goose I'd say).

A short time ago, it was a trend among some so-called "Black" athletes to hold their children in their laps while conducting a post game interview. I never saw white athletes mirror this action. My take on it is that the white athletes look at it as such, "This is my job and I don't need to bring my kids to my job" or to be more exact, "I don't need to front like I'm being a loving, caring dad, I am a loving, caring dad." And it's been said by a wise man that the best gift a man can give his children is to love their mother. Prolific.

You have some Elders who go on these rants in front of rolling news cameras about the state that Afro-people were in back in old America. But if you are an Elder reading this then refer a few paragraphs back and re-read the line about so-called "Blacks" in the old world owning less than 1% of the entire broadcast media system, yet we represent 13% (or more) of the U.S. population. And let's not even talk about communications distribution systems, you know, that thing that the big conglomerate companies are constantly scrambling to maintain control of. Afro-people in the old world were way too comfortable with a white man being at the top of the financial food chain. Ask yourself this: if you read in Forbes magazine that this rapper or that rapper is worth 300 million, How much is the white man worth who signed him? So-called "Black" male rappers act out because the white man will bankroll our plans to display stupidity and the stupider the better. That's not an opinion. That's a fact. If you are an Afro Elder and you have enough money to start a movie company or record label and the distribution system to match (that's a huge task I know) and put out positive images of Afro-people then do so. Otherwise, sit down and shut the fuck up; you're just blowing a bunch of hot air. How can you expect to change a negative image or anything else when you're not willing to put your money where your fat mouth is? If you've been on this earth long enough to be considered an Elder then your Elder statesman or woman status should afford you the wisdom of knowing if you have no financial stake in a certain thing then you are at the mercy of and have to sit and wait on the benevolence of those who do and in this case it's the white people who are trying to maintain their choke hold on all media communications outlets, film, books, t.v., music etc. You can boycott radio stations, record companies, and t.v. networks til you're blue-black in the face, but Cash Rules Everything Around Me—and you too.

Now our motto to the rich in our new Nation is: "Stop being stingy!" We admonish all our great business minds, the well-to-do Afro-people in our nation to network with each other and consolidate their efforts to bring about progress. The new Nation is all about progress. By any means necessary. ;-)

Let's keep moving. We have devised a plan in our new Nation. The entertainment industry (since record, tapes, and CD's have become obsolete) is regulated now by, guess who? You guessed it, the new Nation's government and to be exact, a group of Elders with a specific expertise in various fields of world music study. Long story short, any rapper, spoken-word poet, or musician for that matter who wants to become popular has to be board certified to speak to the people. No more just running to the studio, recording a bunch of dumb-shit about how hard life is for you or what type of ho's you want to bang at the club. I'll admit, if I was a man in my 20's or even early 30's this would be apropos, but at almost forty I don't see white guys, even the ones that like hip-hop, conducting their lives in accordance with the messages in these recordings, but I'd see a bunch of "Black" knuckle-heads living the life every day. There is so much emphasis put on Afro-people to entertain the world, especially Afro-American entertainers—just close your eyes for a moment and think about the number of Afro athletes and music artist you know that have won Grammys or Super Bowl or NBA Championship rings. Now, think of the last time you saw an Afro man win a Nobel Peace Prize for a work in the endeavor of science or a great Afro mathematician. So, we adopted a program with the volunteer help of college statistics graduates and our best legal minds to set up a unified Afro man and woman talent auction. Remember Bo Jackson ("Bo you don't know

Didley"…) and Deon Sanders and even Michael Jordan? What do all three of these men have in common? They're all Afro men. They're all athletes. And all three played more than one professional sport during their careers. And look at Shaq, Allen Iverson, Kobe Bryant, and Ron Artest, all played in the NBA, but all also put out Rap records as well and Waymon Tisdale is a hell of a bass player. Even veteran boxer Roy Jones Jr. took a crack at "rockin'-the-mic". I heard him rap and I guess since his main profession was punchin' dudes in the chin, no one in Roy's camp had the heart to tell him to stick to boxing and leave the rappin' to the professionals. Anyhow, here is our new plan: since the draft process is run much like the auctions for chattel slavery used to be conducted anyway, we say, let's put each "Black" boy up for the highest bidder and hey it's not inhumane because now the Nigger gets paid, whereas in the days of old he might get 40 lashes if he even fixed his face like he didn't dig what was going on around him. You see Negroes now smile and are happy from the door because they know they're going to "GET PAID" big. Sports and music had become like a kind of corporate welfare system for Afro-people in the old America. Our program goes like this, if the NFL wants to contract an Afro athlete they might look him over and say, "Well, we know he can play middle linebacker, but what else can he do? Can he sing, tap-dance, shuffle-off-to-Buffalo, what? And mind you, it is in the Nation's best interest to get the highest amount because the sports team or recording company that contracts them has to pay the Nation a small service fee. Not much, just a teeny-weeny, itty-bitty one. All jokes aside, even this new breed of athletes will be better educated than those in the past because like we said, to be a rapper now you must be board certified by qualified professors of music and poetry and in order for an athlete to play sports during high school or college he or she must maintain, at the very least a 3.0 grade point average in their studies and by that we mean Reading, History and Civics, Science, and Arithmetic not a bunch of basket weaving courses. We, the State, want to hop right on a problem we see as a huge danger to our population. So-called "Black" people in old America made stupid cool and smart un-cool and we, the State, want to greatly increase our nerd quota. We will give new meaning to the term Scholar Athlete. These young men and women will exemplify gladiators not only in body and spirit, but in their mental capacity.

With the mean age for starting a family being between twenty-five and thirty-five years of age, how many Afro men in that age range in old America were at a stage financially, mentally, and emotionally to support a family? Now that I think about it, I've known some grown men who had never moved out of their mamma's house. Ever. An even bigger question is, in old America a natural born citizen of the United States could run for President at age thirty-five. There was this Obama cat, but how many other Afro men of the thirty-five year old age range and above could you say would be qualified to run a nation of only one set of people let alone a melting pot of a bunch of different interests? We are a young nation, but we still try to keep things in perspective. We'll start with our Afro men of thirty-five running a household first then gradually move up to running a nation in due time, although the new Nation was fortunate enough to find some well educated men and women who are sharp, compassionate, and courageous to run our political system. So-called "Blacks" of the old world were so emotional and sensitive, we'd get the argument all the time, "What are you talking about, there are intelligent and competent Afro men that are able to run a country. They're just being held down by 'the man'." Well, in our new world we all can see and experience an Afro man's rule first hand because as Afro men we are all "the man" now. Can you dig it?

The weight of this piece is mostly directed at the men, as it should be, we were put here to take the weight not hide behind a skirt, but hold on fellas. Some responsibility should be taken by Afro women as well. We had a lot of un-wed, "Black" single mothers in the old world and because motherhood had been thrust upon them or they were thrust upon and became mothers, which ever way you want to look at it, Afro-people then mistakenly tended to think that motherhood gave a woman some kind of magical ability to become mature and more intelligent. Hogwash. A theory concocted probably by a "Black" woman. If you were young, dumb, and full of cum before you were impregnated, nine months and a child won't change much except your financial situation may get worse. It seems that a woman may gain a bit of maturity because if she does not have a good family support system, (and hey, if she did why would she disappoint her family, especially her dad and derail a bright future with an unwanted pregnancy?) she is forced into survival mode which makes her have to hustle and maneuver to consolidate money for her and the child and quite often her efforts still come up short. "Charge that to the game" as the ghetto saying goes. Not all pregnancies were a result of poor judgment, some were and still are by design solely on the woman's part and when confronted most may deny it. Consequently, if you are bright enough to figure out how broke you are at any given moment in time and still you purposely act to bring another defenseless person into your misery, you may as well have pushed the kid in front of a 3 ton moving bus because his or her chances of survival are about the same. The circumstance of bearing a child does not boost intellect, but it may prompt a woman to go get more job training or go to college and receive degree for a certain discipline to make her marketability in the work force more appealing. Even once she is able to struggle through and get educated while Grandma or Aunt-tee watches the kid(s) or if she's lucky enough to have enough loot for daycare, often times even with skills Afro women got shuffled into certain types of jobs. I'm thinking of corporate junior executives who usually get put on the fast track for marketing and spokes-person positions in a corporation or in other words a mouth piece for the company, but steered clear of finance departments or anything to do with money. Sales reps or City employees like the enormous amount of Afro women who work for 911 and 411 phone centers in any big city you want to name. Or the inordinate amount of Afro women who work in develop-mental centers and nursing homes. The work places sometimes resembled modern day slavery. These work environments had plenty of Afro female employees, but very few Afro Supervisors or Managers. If we are talking about business professionals, the funny part that no one mentions is the fact that single Afro mothers compete against men and women of all races, ethnicities, and creeds a lot who have chosen not to establish a family so early and most of them are trying to stabilize the foundation of their careers so they can start a family the traditional way. They don't have to worry about dropping a third or more of their weekly paycheck on daycare before even purchasing a home to raise the kid in or being late or having to use a sick day due to a child's illness or just being plain burnt out from the day in and day out stress of raising a child and playing two roles which sets up a "mama sick and tired of being sick and tired" complex. Real families were set up to have each person play his or her role. A lot of Afro-people in the old world were severely confused about what those roles were.

I heard a City Council member give a speech to a group of Graduates at Medgar Evers College in Brooklyn, New York. The Councilman said to them, "A rat or a dog can survive. Human beings were put on earth to thrive." And I might add, be the best and all they can be. It takes two to breed a child, it takes two to raise a child. It takes two to love a child and create a whole productive being. A man. A woman. Anyone who disagrees, DO NOT take your argument up with the author of this. The floor is closed on that subject.

This leads us to the next subject of the new nation. Children. They say it takes a village to raise a child, but if the villages are diseased like most were in old "Black" America then of course the child's out-look on life will be at worse ethically inept and morally bankrupt, and at best a bit tainted with both. In old America there were daytime television shows that centered around family court issues. Usually these court shows had an Afro female judge who quite often came off like old slavery time "mammies". There were a couple of shows with Afro male judges. The saddest sights to see were episodes where a child's paternity is in question. If the results came back negative, you'd see a "Black" man jumping up and down like he just won the lottery and saying idiotic shit like, "I knew it, I knew that kid wasn't mine!" Men are responsible for setting an example of integrity for all of his people. This includes being a living, breathing display of bravery, valor, and good conscience. Not once did I ever see the results come back negative and a "Black" man say to the woman (he obviously slept with at least once), "Even though, I'm not the father, I'll help you as much as I can until you find him" or "If you need my help I'll do what I can." Those court shows prompted a great debate with several Elders, political legislators, and judicial administrators here in the new Nation. It was a great dialogue because the plan we eventually came up with was that all matters of Family court will be over-seen by judges who are married and they will make judgments in more of a tribunal fashion. In divorce cases, child custody battles, or paternity cases there will be a six judges appointed to each case. They will be three sets of man and woman married couple judges and in order to avoid a three on three dead-lock situation all of their rulings must be unanimous. We noticed that singular, un-married judges in the old world were most effective in criminal cases, but not as effective as they could have been in matters concerning family. And the thought process of appointing only man and woman couple married judges is that if you're running a family or have run one and you are also a judge then you can rule from a position of first-hand experience. The process and procedures for divorce in the new world are a bit more intricate than back in the old America and we at this point have a heavy case load for family court administrators, but we are optimistic that these numbers will lower in coming years due to several positive factors that we have put in place recently. In all local municipalities, the county clerk's office where marriage licenses are applied for, we have set up pre-marriage counsel courses and advice sessions conducted by family planning counselors. The courses are optional, but we strongly advise couples to take advantage of them because they are free and very informative. The counselors are highly qualified and paid for by the government and are by law required to have a verifiable, accredited background in psychology and/or sociology. They are to keep their curriculum free of any religious overtones or promotion of any particular affiliation. The courses are conducted by married man/wife couples who have been married for seven years or more. These measures are not to alienate or further deter people who have decided they don't want to be married and have a family, more-so to encourage and help those who do. We are also not so naïve to think we will rid ourselves of divorce completely, we just want to significantly reduce the number of separations and broken homes and upgrade the number of healthy nuclear Afro-families substantially from the ridiculously, pathetic numbers in old America.

As in old America, men who are identified through DNA testing to be the father of a child are required by law to give that child financial support. But unlike the American law the support here lasts until the child's 24th birthday not the 18th. If the man is not able to find work he will be assigned a paid job by his city or county government. Not much pay, but honest work and you'll being doing a service to the community, something you should want to do anyway. Shouldn't be a problem then, right? Right. We will help you help your family, something else you should have a strong desire to do too, right? Right. We'll give you, your wife and children all the food and medical care they need for as long as you are employed by the State. "We'll take care a yous, don't worry, fuuggett aboudditt! "

Now, it is imperative that the woman know who the father of her child is. All the hospitals (even the private ones) are regulated by Federal law. Any woman who shows up to the emergency room in labor must be accompanied by the father of the child unless he is in the armed services or deceased. And we ain't falling for the "he dead and I don't know where they buried 'em " routine. She better know exactly what cemetery and what plot the Nigga is laid in or guess what? If she does not she will be DENIED service and taken to the university medical studies program. Any professional doctor or any other person or persons caught providing mid-wife service to a woman bearing a child without being accompanied by the father of the child will be prosecuted under Federal law, and not only fined, but sentenced to hard labor in a maximum security prison. We ain't fuckin' around. Again all ladies who are expectant mothers are not only to know who their child's father is, but where he is as well. Women alone will no longer be able to apply for Federal and State sponsored food and medical programs without certification of each family member's identity. The State will keep close tabs on Social Security numbers and no more of this using your girlfriend's kid or nieces and nephews to get a bigger tax return. We, the government, don't mind lending a helping hand to one of our own, we understand everyone gets down on their luck sometimes, but there will be a line drawn. In old America Afro women could get what they called food stamps or WIC (Women and Infant Children) only if the man (the biological father of the children or just some nice guy who was bearing the responsibility) is out of the picture. Our new nation only gives the Family money if both man and woman are in the picture. No more of this shit "Oh, he ran away." Our response will be "Ok, go find 'em" and "You won't get a dime from us 'til you do." Or " We'll go look for 'em, if you got a home address, cell phone number, e-mail address, or job address, but the detectives on our payroll start at a G a day and somebody payin' us, either you or him... And we want our bread in cash." Now all this may sound harsh and un-flexible. Yet, if a woman is able to find a man willing to step in as guardian when the biological father has gone we will recognize that. But that would have to be an awfully nice dude because he will have to not only legally adopt the child, but also have intentions to legally marry the woman within 18 months and we will be making note of every day of that 18 months— please believe it. Now to the women readers out there I know some of you may have some challenges in-so-far-as delving into the inner self and taking personal responsibility or accountability for any problems or circumstance we've covered here. Please understand that we the State do not look down kindly upon deadbeat fathers, absolutely no exceptions to the rule. Hence, it will be well noted what we will do to a man if he creates a child then arbitrarily decides to take flight on you. I say that to say this with full knowledge of how we, the Federal gov "gets down" when it comes to punishment for this crime, if your man still decides to break north. That might be more of a reflection on you than him.

The sentiment of one Southern Gentleman who tried to outrun the long arm of the law upon his capture was, "Hey man, y'all can take me to prison or wherever. She don't watch nuttin' but 'Ofrah' and 'Tyrah—Ofrah Jr.' and soap operas, and them out-of-control, white broads on 'Sex All Over The City' and them equally out-of-control, "Black" broads on 'Galfriends', as if we needed a "Black" version of that shit. Or that damn show 'Conniving Housewives' and you cain't tell her nothing. Head hard as a brick. She know evrythang and she ain't neva wrong. She won't even pick up a book and read about Ancient Queens in Africa and how their knowledge and understanding Mothered civilization. And to top that off, I cain't even run my fangas thu her hair 'cause they gets all tangled up in all the damn weave, that's why two of 'em in a splint now. Hey, man, take me please, if you gotta kill me, kill me. I just don't want to have to deal with her no more. Do me a fava an' jus' drop me off at the nutt-house... any nutt-house, please."

There was a poster that poignantly illustrates what our new Nation seeks to rid itself of. In the poster there was a homeless Afro-man of prime age out on the sidewalk and the caption at the top read: "SAD, THIS BLACK MAN IS HOMELESS WHILE SO MANY BLACK HOMES ARE MANLESS." One might think these new laws are a bit restricting, yet abortion will still be legal. Furthermore, the man is offered a measure of protection in the form of an Opt-Out agreement between him and the State. If he has sex with a woman un-protected or if there is some malfunction with the contraception method used and he even suspects he has gotten her pregnant. He can go to the local authorities and tell them his situation. If he tells the woman he has had sex with that he does not want a child at this time and that she is on her own, they both have an obligation to inform the State of their situation. Well-to-do families will be able to cover this up pretty smoothly, but for everyone else, trust me, you're going to want to follow the rules. The woman will be summoned to have a pregnancy test, paid for by us, to determine if she is or isn't with child and a DNA test to determine if the man in question is or isn't the father. After 16 weeks though, abortions can not be performed. And if you are on the fence about the whole thing and loose track of time and come forward after that 16 week time frame, weather you are the biological father or not, as far as the State's concerned, "You da' Pappy now!" Time is of the essence, so the sooner one or both alerts us the better off things will be in the end. In other words, if we have to come looking for you, you're not going to like it when we find you. And we will find you.

Conversely, a man who chooses to abide by the law and be a productive citizen and create a healthy family base will be greatly rewarded. One thing our government will offer is a cash back tax credit on every child the man has in his custody up to four in number. Our country's great mathematical minds have discovered that at this time four is about the number the average household, bringing in an average income between an adult man and woman can handle without putting a strain on the county's central bank. We also offer to men between the ages of twenty-six and fifty-six years of age who have four kids a FREE vasectomy, but don't worry we're not going to send you to the university student doctors, we've had a few mishaps and… well,… never-mind…We've got the situation under control now. We have MD's experienced in that sort of thing—when it comes to that nothing but the best, top shelf all the way, baby. Now that's not to say you can't have five or more kids if you want, Playa. We just look to discourage this kind of thing especially for those with incomes well below the mean average. And for those young 'uns that 'oops', accidentally start a family before the age of twenty-one, the State will send someone 'round to give both sets of parents a stern talking to about how to talk to your teenagers about sex. In the end we're sure you'll see things our way. The State employs nothing but the best when it comes to agents knowledgeable of tactics of persuasion. Some of those tactics may be of the five knuckle type, but you didn't hear that from me.

A woman who refuses to abide by the law will be allowed to give birth in a humane fashion. There's the University hospitals for newly graduated doctors still in residency to perfect their child delivery skills, but it should also be noted that the University doctors really don't want to be there because they are not paid for their service. They're practicing—on you. Depending on what time of day you give birth, you may get an A student or you may get a D student, it's the luck of the draw. Now before a lot of readers start bitchin' & moanin' about how this looks like we're coming down on single Afro mother's, we also don't want Afro men raising kids alone either. With the laws we have in place the only way we see as an out for you if you're married with kids is if your spouse drops dead. It has been brought to our attention that the spousal murder rate may climb, but we'll cross that bridge when we come to it.

For those Afro women who refuse to comply, upon delivery, the nurses will take the child and the mother will not be allowed to see it. Arrangements will be made to place the child in a permanent home with a Mother and Father, but first, the biological mother will be given up to 30 months to show some progress in educating herself and become a productive member of society who is able to run or help run the business of a raising a family. During the 30 month period, she will be given a State job with monies going directly to her child in a State run orphanage. Hopefully, during that time she will be able to go out into society and paint herself into a picture of a harmonious, productive family life. If she is unsuccessful, then the family that has given the child a home during the 30 months has an option to keep the child or the child may be given back. He or she will then become award of the State and held until they are able to be placed in a home permanently. In the unfortunate event that the kid is just too ugly or dumb or a combination of ugly and dumb to be adopted, all is not lost. The most likely option is the child will be taken from the orphanage and sent at the age of five to a military academy and raised there and then groomed to become a member of one of the branches of the armed service. No offense to any service people, but ugly, dumb people do make better fighters on the front line—they got nothing to loose. Unlike the laws and statutes in the old America, a child will be able to find records of their biological parents well before their 18th birthday. The logic being that once your own child is able to talk and develop thought, maybe they can persuade you to do enough to build a reasonably safe environment for them albeit that you are attempting to do it after-the-fact of their arrival on earth, but better late than never we say, and better you than us.

If you're like me, you probably think throwing a kid in the army is just foul and a horrible way to treat them just for being born into a messed up circumstance, but I would bet there are a lot of homeless, junkies, prostitutes, strippers, pimps, and drug dealers who wish they weren't born into the circumstances they've had to endure as well. Maybe the thought has even crossed their mind at some point, "I'm here and it's up to me to figure out why because it doesn't look like the two people that brought me here thought this thing through." Some people are left to their own devices to define themselves with no guidance from knowledgeable, parental figures and most times the results are disastrous, just refer to any gangster rapper who said he or she dealt drugs or stripped to survive before he or she rapped and it should be clear.

We here in the new Nation want to do our very best to be a progressive and positive force on planet earth. We anticipate that people will misunderstand our noble intentions in the beginning. We are anti-crime, especially crime committed by our people against our people. Charity begins at home, so does discipline. From the tone of this some may think we are anti-white people. We are not. If anything we admire them and are envious of the order and organizational expertise they have with banking institutions, libraries, public records, museums, and the parliamentary process with which they run their government. Yet, we are anti-white supremacy. The Most High Creator created us all equal and no one type of people should be looked upon as supreme or dominate to any other type of people, but if you take a look around the world and see the way the countries of little Europe try to dominate the bigger countries (in population and land mass) of the world, you get the idea that some people actually do think they can rule the world. They own fifty percent of the world's weapons of mass destruction. We are in awe of the raw aggression with which white America administers a swift smack-down to any adversary or foe that stands in the way of their progress. Sometimes we don't know weather to applaud their armed forces' efficient ass-kicking technique or shake our heads in shame at the play-ground bully?

One thing we know is that to create a great Nation you must first cultivate great individuals. Great individuals beget Great families, Great families beget Great neighborhoods, Great neighborhoods beget Great cities, Great cities beget Great Nations, and Great Nations create a better world. And it all starts from a single, individual person.

These new ideas may scare some "Black" and "White" alike, but just remember this not reality.

Yet.

It's all just a dream for a New Afro Nation.

P.S.

If you thought this was brilliant then I'll gladly take the title of Genius.

On the other hand, if you thought this was the most idiotic thing you've ever heard of in your life and the ramblings of a complete lunatic then just ignore me—I haven't had my medication today.

Father   Mother

Son   Daughter
"Brother"   "Sister"

AFTER WORD

This is clearly not a book on dating or relationships, but it is a story about how we relate to one another. The grid on the previous page has the four members of a family inside a 360 degree circle. I drew stick figures so you can see all you need to do is take pencil and paper and draw these people and label their title/position in your life then look at the lines of connection you have with each and what they add up to for you. They say for a boy, your Mom is your first girlfriend and for a girl, your Dad is your first boyfriend. Family is how we are socialized into the world and also how we learn to communicate and become connected to world around. If family is a system then with so many absentee Afro-fathers and over-burdened mothers our system has serious a glitch.

We may not like a particular president, but we still call him Mr. President when he is in office (we may call him a bunch of other things 'expletive deleted' behind closed doors) but for the most part we show respect for the office he holds.

Maybe we could look at our Mothers and Fathers that way too. As positions that are in one sense symbolic. Titles. Once we add definition to the titles then maybe we can get a clearer picture of what we can or can't or should or should not expect from the people who hold these offices. We may be better able to differentiate a Father from a man who is just a sperm donor or a Mother from a woman who quite simply supplied her womb to the cause of acting as a vessel for a human fetus. There is a distinct difference between humankind and animals and an even bigger difference between Men and Women and

Kings and Queens.

I once worked with a guy who told me his Mom had abandoned him and his dad on Christmas Eve when he was eight. As our shift went on we kept talking and he started telling me about the relationship he was in at the time. I remember him saying, "I love my Baby's-Mother, but I don't trust her." I remember thinking if there is anybody in this world you should be able to trust it's her. But I never said anything.

Am I over-simplifying things by drawing a parallel from the experience the man had with his mother to the problems he had with his child's mother? Possibly. But it is here and can not be ignored. I have long since moved on from that job, but before I had left, I heard that he had married his son's mother and they bought a home together.
I was happy for him and hope that they are still a unit and happy.

When a man thinks about the woman he wants to be with what are his expectations? Are they too high and unrealistic? Or are they lowered to the point that almost any chick will be able to just step over the bar? If your best friend moves from one woman to the next and his only criteria: cute face, big ass, nice breasts and sometimes he'll sacrifice all three for panties and a pulse and if he enjoys that lifestyle, it'll do you good to just listen and laugh when he spins his stories of conquest, but take nothing to heart. If you are looking for something stable, your friend is not the one to ask for advice on women. He is lost too and it will just be the blind leading the blind if you think he may be able to council you. It works the same way for a woman, is it good enough that a man just looks the part? What tool do you have to size him up? His integrity, his honor, his compassion. If Daddy, Grand-daddy, Uncle, Older brother, or Mom's good male friend wasn't around as a yard stick, you have nothing. If your Mamma, Auntees, and Sisters don't have or can't keep a man they're no help to you. And if all the Afro-men around you seem morally mis-guided, emotionally absent, or just somebody you don't ever see yourself (or for that matter any child that may be produced by you and him) learning anything worthwhile from then it seems, if you Love Afro-men, you are between a rock and a hard place.

You have people who either move from relationship to relationship or choose an "alternative" lifestyle and still move from relationship to relationship because they are either lost or never taught how to develop healthy behavior patterns to relate to and associate with the opposite sex and it is in these relationships the Greatest and only precious natural resource is made, the Human resource.

When I went out on dates I made a point of asking about her (whoever her was at the moment) relationship with her Father, thinking this would be a gauge for how much trouble I might be in for if the relationship lasted for the long haul. My mistake was I discounted the fact that each woman had varying degrees of having resolved whatever childhood issues there were in her life and sometimes I hit the red flag button too quick. Some were a lot further along than me. A couple had achieved a kind of closure and were moving on, but most had not even begun to think about what their past meant, so they kept chasing tomorrow and not realizing the hurt of right now doesn't go away on it's own, you're going to have to have a "Moment of Truth" and seriously reflect on yesterday, not to sulk, get depressed, or dwell on the past negatives, but honestly and objectively look at them and see how they can be transmuted to a positive present. Keep in mind that while you are on the path to seek TRUTH, you can't force anyone else confront it and it's not absolutely necessary.

If a relationship is a house—when two people meet they track in a certain amount of dirt (you can call it baggage too). I learned over time not to be so concerned about her camouflaging something that may be a problem down the line or anticipate or predict an outcome too hastily. If you can honestly figure you out then you will attract the energy you give off. Scared, nervous energy attracts scared, nervous energy and conversely calm, peaceful energy attracts calm, peaceful energy—it's the way of the world. If a man or a woman has problems that they keep bottled inside and stay isolated in their apartments or homes, those are personal problems. The second they come out and compare and contrast what they think and feel to others and discover a commonality of being effected similarly by the relative conditions of the world around them, those become social problems. Many highly intelligent sociologists and psychologists have studied the effect that slavery has had on Afro-people and the remaining scars it has left, evident in the way we behave toward one another. It is not my area of expertise, so I will leave that to the Henry Louis Gates Jr.'s and Cornel West's of the world.

The wisdom of elders is priceless. A bride and groom were wed by the Bride's grandfather in his church. He prayed for them at the ceremony and blessed their marriage. As a wedding gift he gave them the last two pieces of an heirloom set of precious China tea cups. He told them they were extremely rare and that since there were only two left they could think of them as him and her cups. One cup pictured a young man and woman holding hands under a Cherry blossom tree around the other side of the cup the same couple stood side by side on a mountain top dressed in regal garb like King and Queen. The other cup had a little boy and little girl splashing water in a pond with swans lazily swimming in the background and in the faint distance around the other side of the cup was the couple from the first cup looking on at the children play. The young bride and groom both were very hard workers and struggled in the early years of their marriage to maintain finances and other day to day details connected to managing a household. Always when there was a problem or concern either the Groom's Mother was there or the Bride's Grandfather. Times had gotten to the worst point between the couple about six years into their marriage. The couple invited her Grandfather over to Sunday dinner and right away he could sense something was wrong between the couple. After dinner they all sat in the living room and they did not discuss any particular problems, but the vibe in the room was heavy and the couple finally told the Grandfather that they planned to separate. He sat silent for a long time and stared straight ahead. His gaze was far off and distant. He was somewhere else. After a while he broke the silence and the couple realized that her was staring at the China cabinet. "Those tea cups are beautiful aren't they?" The Grandfather said.

"Yes", the couple replied almost in unison.

"You know they are priceless. There will be no more after this, these are the last", he continued. "I have something to help your marriage, a big big gift." The couple looked at each other and anticipated what it could be. He had already given them so much over the years not just monetarily, but helpful advise with his wisdom and insight on life that they would feel guilty taking even another dime of his money. He took out his handkerchief and walked over to the China cabinet and as he did, he started re-telling the story of how he met his wife and how he knew they would one day be married. The Grandfather reached inside the cabinet and took out the two prize tea cups a wrapped them inside his handkerchief. The couple looked on and always enjoyed him re-telling stories they had heard a million times, but each re-telling he would seem to add a funny detail that wasn't in his last recount of the tale. He placed the handkerchief on the floor with the cups inside. He stomped with his heel smashing the tea cups to tiny bits. The couple's smiles were frozen on their faces, but it was because they didn't know what to say or do next. The cups were rare, one of a kind. The Grandfather looked over at them and smiled, "You are both waiting for the gift, right?" They tried to keep smiling and shrugged their shoulders "yes". The Grandfather went into the kitchen underneath the sink and pulled out a bottle of glue. He brought it back into the living room and gave it to the couple. They both thanked him, but he explained that the glue was not the gift. He told them the gift he had was really really big, but that he could not give it to them just yet, he made up some excuse. He told the couple to make a game of gluing the two cups back together. He said the next time I see you two, you will have both these cups together and I will have your gift.

"But Grand-dad the cups won't be the same. We won't be able to do anything with them" His Grand-daughter chimed in.

The Grandfather joked, "Nonsense, you'll be able to do the exact same thing you always did with them... Look at them.... And you're right they won't be the same - they'll be better" The couple knew the Grandfather was getting old and he always seemed to be in his right mind, but tonight they both started to wonder if the first stages of dementia were setting in. Time went on and the couple did as the Grandfather had instructed and started gluing the tea cups back together. Months went by and Grandfather would come by and ask how far along the tea cups were and they would show him. In their spare time the couple would sit for a while and identify pieces then glue them in place and after a few more months they decided to buy a paint set to try to recapture the essence of the original pictures. Sometimes they would talk as they worked other times they would sit side by side in silence for a couple of hours, re-building. A couple of years later, once they had completed putting the cups back together, they placed them back in the China cabinet and laughed about the fact that the cups no longer looked right-out-of-the-box as they had when Grandfather had given them, but in a strange way he was right they did look better. The Grandfather stopped by one Sunday afternoon and brought the gift he had promised. He gave them a box and as he did he told them, "The gift is for you and not for you." They opened the box to find a set of four tea cups exactly like the ones he had given them as a wedding gift. The husband took the original tea cups out of the cabinet and looked on the inside of the finger handle and could see it read: 'Made in Mexico'. "I thought you said these were one of a kind?", the husband said.

"I said they were priceless and since I was the one giving them to you they were. And I said they were the last... The last of a set of four." He chuckled. "Now you can take these new ones and give them as a wedding gift to one of your children and tell them anything you want."

What the Afro-people in America need is a balanced Father-Mother energy that encompasses the strength of discipline, wisdom, and compassion. It doesn't matter who is President or what color they are, if the people are not right within themselves they will continue to be needy and seek to hang all their worries and woes on a savior or messiah figure and sadly become angry at him if and when he can't come through. Afro-people have to grow up and truly understand the meaning of individual responsibility which goes well beyond just going to the polls and voting for the first Afro-President and throwing a party because he won.

It does pay to examine your origins and have a clear line of sight to who you are and where you came from and that will give you clarity on who you are suppose to be and where you are going. The people holding the offices of Mother or Father in your life are not to be judged or compared to others even if they have not made wise choices in regards to your life or their own. The most important thing for each individual is to be able to as best they can UNDERSTAND, FORGIVE, CORRECT and move forward.

S.C. Gunn 11-21-08

DEDICATED
To my lifeline and support system my Mom and younger brother from another mother, Roderick. Many thanks to my family and friends. Ken for the many conversations over the years. Youghnese and Susan for being sisters and listening. My other brother from another mother and West Coast connec, Carlos.

INFLUENCES
Richard Pryor, August Wilson, and William Faulkner.

INSPIRATIONS
"A Modest Proposal" by Jonathan Swift, "A Clockwork Orange" by Anthony Burgess, "Fear And Loathing On The Campaign Trail 1972" by Hunter S. Thompson, "Faces at the Bottom of the Well" by Derrick Bell.

SUGGESTED READING LIST (in this order):

Note: If any or all of these books are not immediately available or out-of-print—FIND THEM. You may want to start your search on-line at www.alibris.com or www.bookfinder.com.

1 "Pimps, Whores, and Welfare Brats" by Star Parker

2 "The Black Man's Guide to Understanding the Black Woman" by Shahrazad Ali

3 "In Search of Goodpussy" by Don Spears

4 "The Endangered Black Family" by Nathan Hare, Ph.D and Julia Hare Ed.D

5 "All God's Children: The Bosket Family and the American Tradition of Violence" by Fox Butterfield

6 "Killing the Black Body - Race, Reproduction, and the meaning of Liberty" by Dorothy Roberts

In this age of easy access and information over-load, develop your own methods to sharpen your skills at breaking down information—observing, analyzing, and extracting all the useful content to find truth. This will set you on a path and the reading list is just a suggested starting point. May the MOST HIGH CREATOR be with you on your journey.

www.ingramcontent.com/pod-product-compliance
Lightning Source LLC
Chambersburg PA
CBHW071214130626
46555CB00004B/1703